FOOTBALL ZOOM

Written by Hazel Townson
Illustrated by Philippe Dupasquier

GINN

Ziggy Zoom saw Jan and Tim.
They were playing football.

'Come and play football, Ziggy,' said Jan.

'Yes. Come and play,' said Tim.

Come on.

Big Bert yelled, 'No! He can't play!'

'He can't play,' Big Bert yelled again.
'He's got wheels.'

'I'm the ref,' shouted Tim.
'And I say he can play.'

Come on,
Ziggy.

Ziggy played football.

He went very fast and . . .

he scored all the goals.

Big Bert went mad.
He ran after Ziggy.

His team went after him too.

Ziggy jumped over the fence.

He went faster and faster . . .

until he got to a big wall.

'Ha! Ha! You can't get over that wall,'
said Big Bert.

'Oh, yes I can!' said Ziggy and he went zoom . . .

He went zoom over the wall.